WRITTEN BY

Gretchen Brandenburg McLellan

WHEN YOUR DADDY'S A SOLDIER

ILLUSTRATED BY

EG Keller

VIKING

VIKING
An imprint of Penguin Random House LLC, New York

First published in the United States of America by Viking,
an imprint of Penguin Random House LLC, 2022

Visit us online at penguinrandomhouse.com.

Library of Congress Cataloging-in-Publication Data is available.

Manufactured in China

ISBN 9780593463901

1 3 5 7 9 10 8 6 4 2

TOPL

Edited by Liza Kaplan
Design by Monique Sterling
Text set in Adobe Caslon

Artwork created with Procreate on an iPad.

For my sisters and brother and military brats everywhere —G. B. M.

For Dad —E. K.

When your daddy's a soldier like mine, you want to be a soldier, too.

You wear camo like he does. You wear dog tags like he does. And you want to ride in a tank or a helicopter just like he does, too.

chk chk chk chk chk chk

When your daddy comes home from work,
you race to unlace his big boots and yank
and pull until they pop off.

You put them on and march around while his happy toes wiggle.

But sometimes, your daddy doesn't get to come home from work. Sometimes he has to go away, and you can't be with him. When he tells you this, you want to stick your fingers in your ears and never take them out.

When your daddy's a soldier, sometimes he gets ordered
to work far, far away, for a maybe-forever long time.

Our daddy is going to war.

Sis cries, but I try to act like a soldier. Brave.
Daddy says he's proud of me, but his voice sounds lumpy.

Later I hide in my fort and cry.

Before Daddy leaves, he places his favorite hat on my head. Then he tells me I'm the man of the house now and to take good care of Mama and Sis.

But after he's gone, I don't sit in his place at the table. His chair is so empty my throat hurts. Sis still sets a place for him. Mama doesn't eat. I tell her a joke to make her smile. Then Sis does, too.

When your daddy's a soldier far away at war, your mama's not the same. Sometimes it seems like she's gone, too. Sometimes you have to jump up and down before she even knows you're talking. Sometimes she expects you to be all grown up, and others, she acts like you're a baby again.

And sometimes you do things you did
when you were really little, like twirl your
finger around and around in your hair.
Or sleep with your lights on again.

We draw pictures and write letters to Daddy.
My class writes letters, too. We thank him for
his service and invite him to visit our school
when he comes home.

Daddy writes back that he puts
the letters up where he can see
them—right next to our pictures.
His buddies say he's lucky to have
such a great family.

We send him other things, too.

Sis sends her favorite seashell so Daddy
won't forget the sound of our ocean.

I send him a skipping stone to carry in his pocket. Daddy and I
found it right before he left and promised to watch it fly when
he gets home. I don't want him to forget.

I tell Mama I want to mail myself, too. Then Sis copies me.
Mama laughs and says we can bake his favorite cookies instead.

When your daddy's a soldier like mine, a day comes that's better than all your birthdays and holidays put together. That's the day you hear that your daddy is coming home.

At the airport we wait and
wait and wait for Daddy.
And then we see him! Sis
and I take off running.

And then Mama is there, and I don't think she will ever stop kissing him. When they finally stop, Daddy spins Sis in a hug around and around and then swings me up on his shoulders. Together we are bigger than anyone in the whole wide world.

At home, Daddy's chair is full again, and we have fun, fun, fun!

We have a slumber party and play games and eat
lots of ice cream. Daddy can't get enough ice cream.
He says the war is always hot.

Daddy tells us he's proud of the way we've taken care of one another while he's been gone. He says we should get a medal for keeping our family strong.

Daddy gives us camo backpacks with his mission and unit patches on them. I show mine off to everyone at school.

My teacher asks me how I'm feeling. "Happy," I say. "My daddy's home!" "That's joy, honey. JOY." And her eyes shine.

When Daddy visits our school, we have a special assembly to honor him and all veterans. Sis and I stand tall next to Daddy on the stage.

But when your daddy's a soldier, he doesn't get to stay home for good. He has to go back to his unit. Back to the war.

This time when he leaves, Daddy holds me so tight that I don't think either of us will ever let go. Daddy makes a joke about me being Velcro boy and peels me off. Softly, he says, "Chin up, son. I'll be home again."

He ruffles my hair, shoulders his bag, and walks away.

Then he turns around one last time and waves goodbye.

When your daddy's a soldier like mine, you wish you were big enough and brave enough to be a soldier, too, so you could always stay together.

For now, you do your best to be brave and strong during the day. You pray that your daddy will come home soon.

And at night, you dream of peace.